Ladybird  Readers

Under the Oceans

Series Editor: Sorrel Pitts
Text adapted by Sorrel Pitts
Illustrated by Stephanie Fizer Coleman

LADYBIRD BOOKS

UK | USA | Canada | Ireland | Australia
India | New Zealand | South Africa

Ladybird Books is part of the Penguin Random House group of companies
whose addresses can be found at global.penguinrandomhouse.com.
www.penguin.co.uk   www.puffin.co.uk   www.ladybird.co.uk

Penguin
Random House
UK

First published 2017
001

Copyright © Ladybird Books Ltd, 2017

Printed in China

A CIP catalogue record for this book is available from the British Library

ISBN: 978-0-241-29888-6

All correspondence to
Ladybird Books
Penguin Random House Children's
80 Strand, London WC2R 0RL

MIX
Paper from
responsible sources
FSC
www.fsc.org
FSC® C018179

Under the Oceans

Contents

Picture words

angler fish

blue whale

blue-ringed
octopus

cuttlefish

giant clam

giant spider
crab

tentacles

giant squid

gulper eel

stinger

jellyfish

spine

scorpion fish

stargazer fish

rock pool

Wonderful world

The world is wonderful, and most of it is sea. We call our big seas 'oceans'.

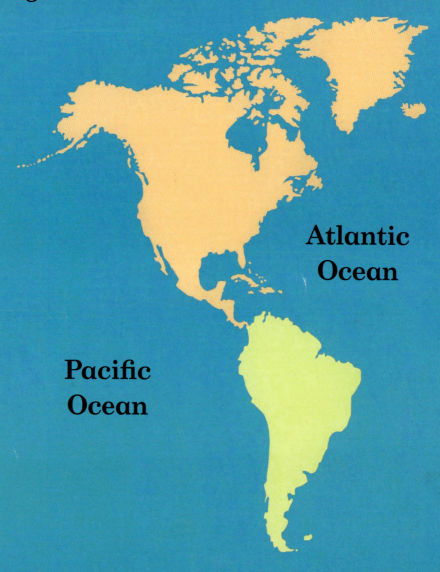

Atlantic Ocean

Pacific Ocean

Here are the oceans. Many animals in the world live in the oceans.

Arctic Ocean

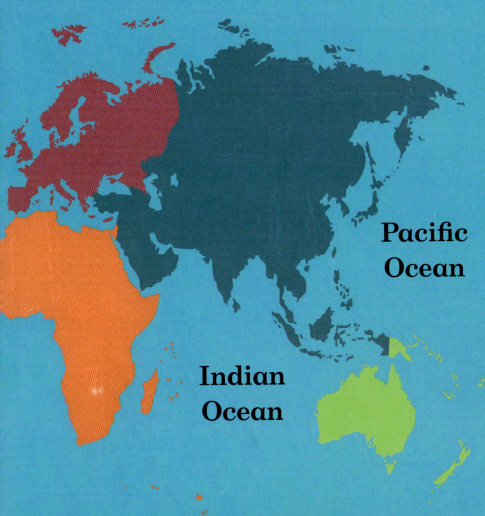

Pacific
Ocean

Indian
Ocean

Southern Ocean

Rock pools

When there is not much water on a beach, you can sometimes see rock pools.

There are lots of small animals and plants in rock pools.

Look carefully in the rock pool. What can you see?

Which animals can you
see in this rock pool?

Coral reefs

You can find coral in clean water that is not cold or deep.

Coral looks like rock, but is made of lots of very small animals.

Lots of coral becomes a reef, like this.

Many small fish live on coral reefs.

coral reefs

There are coral reefs in the Atlantic,
Pacific, and Indian Oceans.

13

Animals that hide

There are lots of small animals on coral reefs, but you cannot see them!

They look like plants, so that other animals do not eat them.

Some fish can look like rocks,
so that they can hide. When other
fish come near, the fish that is
hiding quickly eats them!

Jellyfish

If you swim away from the coral reef, you may see jellyfish.

Jellyfish live in all the oceans. Be careful. Some jellyfish have got stingers!

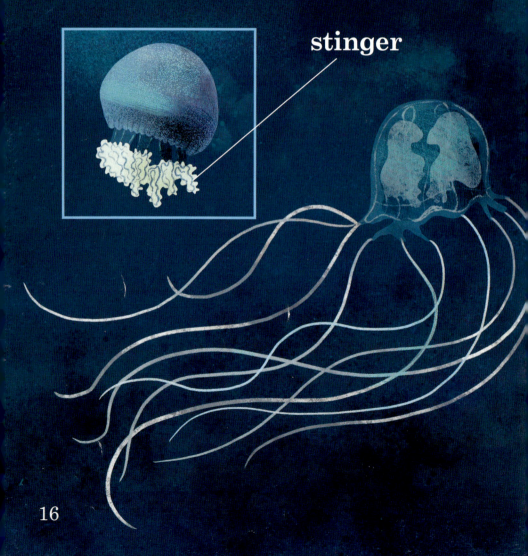

stinger

There are many different jellyfish.
Some of them have many colors.

Spines and stingers

Lots of animals and fish in the
oceans have spines and stingers.

Scorpion fish have very thin spines.
They use the spines to sting
other animals.

spine

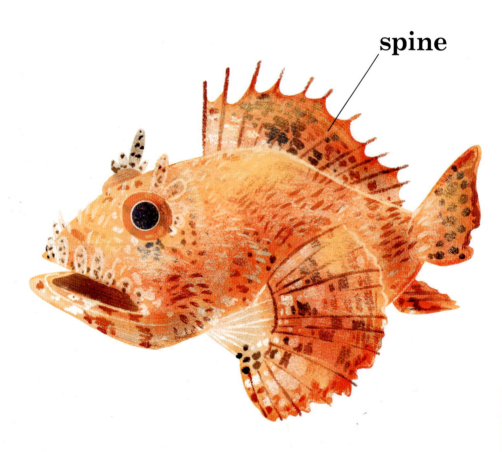

Stargazer fish have an
electric stinger.

The electric stinger is on
the top of a stargazer fish.

Animals with shells

Many animals in the oceans do not have spines or stingers.

A giant spider crab has a hard shell, so other animals cannot eat it easily.

giant spider crab

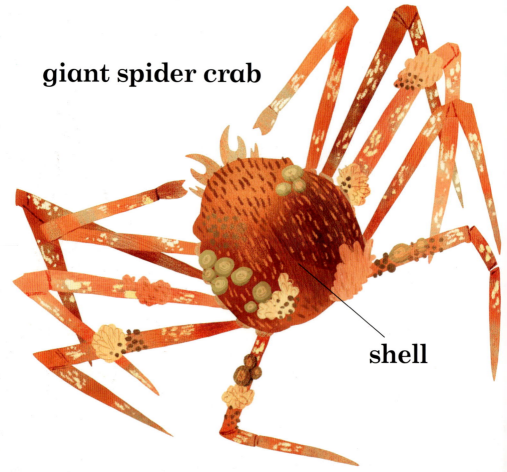

shell

Very small animals live on the giant spider crab's shell.

Giant clams have big, hard shells, which are many different colors.

giant clam

Lots of very small plants live in the clam.

Animals that change color

Some animals, like the blue-ringed octopus, can change color.

blue-ringed octopus

The colors of a blue-ringed octopus become bright, and then they change!

The skin of a cuttlefish can show many colors at the same time.

cuttlefish

Cuttlefish can change color
to hide from other fish.

Big squid

A giant squid has long arms and two very long tentacles. The arms and tentacles catch other animals for the squid to eat.

Can you see the squid's big eyes?

Giant squid have the biggest eyes in the world!

tentacles

giant squid

Giant squid live in
all the world's oceans.

Big teeth

Do not go too close!
Most sharks have big teeth.

Some sharks eat small animals.
This shark eats big animals and
other sharks.

big teeth

Sharks can grow very big,
but they are not the biggest
animals in the ocean.

This is a very long shark!

The biggest animals in the world

Blue whales are the biggest animals in the world. They are 30 meters long!

Blue whales eat lots and lots of very tiny animals.

blue whale

The bottom of the oceans

Near the bottom of the oceans, it is very dark and very cold.

The animals that live near the bottom of the oceans like the cold, and no light.

Many of them look very different from other animals in the oceans!

Many of the animals at the bottom
of the oceans look very strange!

A light in the dark

Some fish that live in the dark oceans can make a bright light. Angler fish and gulper eels do this.

angler fish

Angler fish have a light here.

Fish swim close to the light — and the angler fish eats them!

You can find gulper eels in all the world's oceans.

gulper eel

Fish swim close — and the gulper eel eats them!

Gulper eels have a light here.

New animals

New animals are still found
in the oceans.

This is a ninja shark. It has very
dark skin, which helps it to hide
from other fish. But its skin
becomes a light in the dark ocean
when it is looking for food.

ninja shark

The ninja shark was found in the Pacific
Ocean near Central America in 2015.

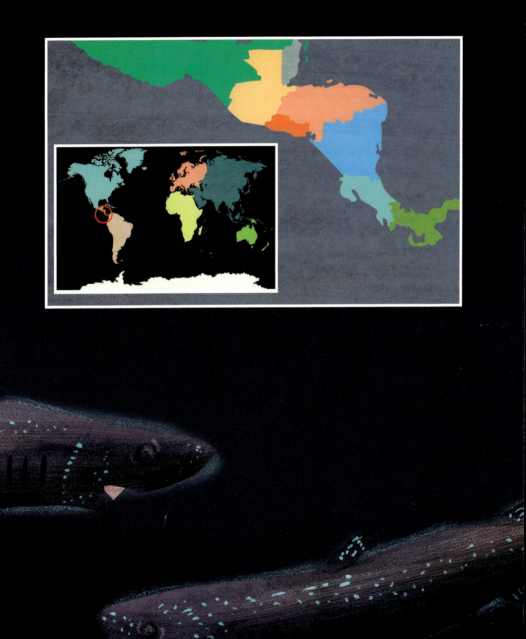

Problems in the oceans

There are many problems for the animals and plants that live in the oceans.

People catch fish to eat, and for other people to eat. But if people catch too many fish, there may not be enough of them in the future.

We must not catch
too many fish!

Garbage in the oceans

One of the biggest problems in the oceans is garbage — the things people don't want, like plastic bottles. Fish and other animals eat the garbage because to them it looks good to eat.

Plastic garbage is found in all
the oceans.

plastic bottles

What can we do?

We can clean the beaches and the oceans.

Make sure you collect your garbage from the beach.

We could make a machine like this.
It could find garbage in the water.

cleaning machine

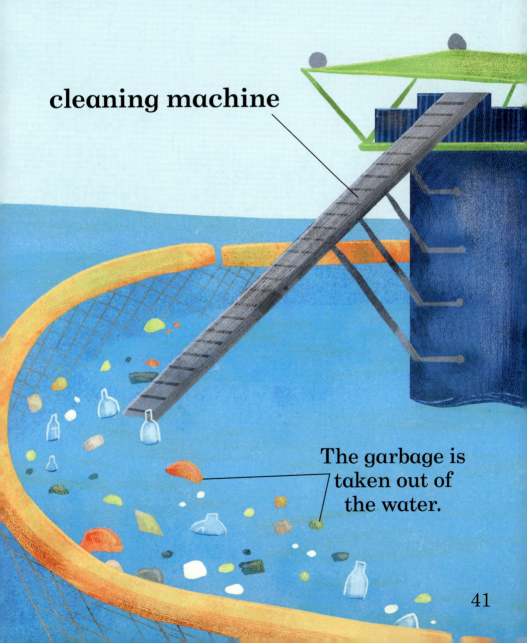

The garbage is taken out of the water.

Looking after the oceans

The oceans are wonderful.

We have to care for them, or we may lose all the animals and plants that live in them.

We have to look after the oceans now.

Activities

The key below describes the skills practiced in each activity.

Spelling and writing

Reading

Speaking

Critical thinking

Preparation for the Cambridge Young Learners Exams

1 **Look and read. Choose the correct words and write them on the lines.** 📖 ✏️ ⭐

| coral | jellyfish | ocean | scorpion fish |

1 A big area of water is called this. .... ocean ....

2 This looks like rock but is made from lots of very small animals. ....

3 Lots of these fish have stingers, and they live in all the oceans. ....

4 These fish have very thin spines. ....

2 **Look, match, and write the words.**

1	ninja		whale
2	blue		crab
3	giant		shark
4	spider		clam

1 ninja shark

2 ....

3 ....

4 ....

3 Look and read. Put a ✓ or a ✗ in the boxes. 📖 ❓ 🌼

1  You can always find rock pools on beaches.

2  Everything in a rock pool can swim.

3 When the ocean comes up the beach, the fish in the rock pools swim away.

4 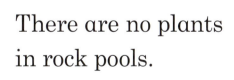 There are no plants in rock pools.

5  Big fish also live in rock pools.

4 **Look and read. Write the missing words.** 📖 ✏️

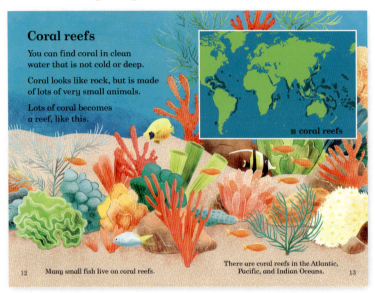

Coral reefs

You can find coral in clean water that is not cold or deep.

Coral looks like rock, but is made of lots of very small animals.

Lots of coral becomes a reef, like this.

■ coral reefs

12   Many small fish live on coral reefs.

There are coral reefs in the Atlantic, Pacific, and Indian Oceans.   13

coral   small   deep   clean

1 Coral is not found in ⸺ deep ⸺ water.

2 Many small fish live on ⸺⸺⸺ reefs.

3 Coral looks like rock, but is made up of very ⸺⸺⸺ animals.

4 Coral is found in ⸺⸺⸺ water.

5 **Match the two parts of the sentences.** 📖

1 There are lots of small animals on coral reefs,

2 They look like plants, so that other animals

3 Some fish can look like rocks,

4 When other fish come near,

5 Animals that hide on coral reefs

a do not eat them.

b are safe from hungry animals.

c the fish that is hiding quickly eats them!

d but you cannot see them!

e so that they can hide.

49

6 **Talk to a friend about coral reefs.**

1 **Where can you find coral reefs?**

You can find them in clean water that is not deep.

2 What is coral made of?

3 Which oceans have coral reefs?

4 What lives on coral reefs?

7 **Read and circle the correct verbs.**

1 Some fish can (look like)/ look after rocks.

2 When other fish come near, the fish that is **hide / hiding** quickly eats them!

3 If you swim in the oceans, you **won't / may** see jellyfish.

4 New animals are still **find / found** in the oceans.

5 The ninja shark **found / was found** in the Pacific Ocean in 2015.

8 **Look at the letters. Write the words.** 📖 🖊

1 (l e f y i j s l h)

If you swim away from the coral reef, you may see <u>jellyfish</u>.

2 (e a s n o c)

Jellyfish live in all the _____.

3 (r c o s l o)

Some jellyfish have many _____.

4 (s t s g e i n r)

Some jellyfish have got _____!

5 (c f a u r l e)

Be _____! Jellyfish stings really hurt.

9 **Read the text. Choose the correct words and write them next to 1—5.**

> stingers spines sting
> stargazer fish   scorpion fish

Lots of animals and fish in the oceans have spines and [1] stingers .
They may sting you when you swim too near. [2] _____ have very thin spines. They use the spines to [3] _____ other animals.
[4] _____ have an electric stinger.
[5] _____ and stingers help to frighten other animals away.

10 **Circle the correct pictures.**

1 The skin of this animal can show many colors at the same time.

2 This animal can change color.

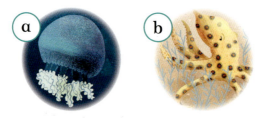

3 This animal is the biggest in the world.

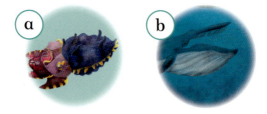

4 This big animal has long arms and two very long tentacles.

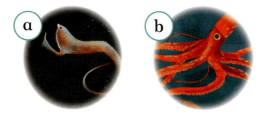

Choose the correct words, and write them on the lines. 📖 🖊 ✿

1 Scorpion fish have very
_____thin_____ spines.
a small **b** (thin)

2 Stargazer fish have an
_____ stinger.
a electric **b** giant

3 A giant spider crab has a
_____ shell, so other
animals can't eat it easily.
a bright **b** hard

4 The colors of the blue-ringed
octopus become _____,
and then they change!
a bright **b** hard

55

12 **Match the words to the pictures.**

1 stinger

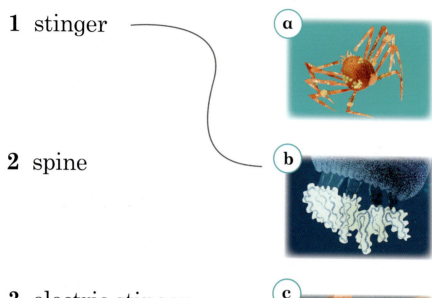

2 spine

3 electric stinger

4 shell

5 tentacles

13 Put the animals in the correct boxes in the table.

angler fish

giant clam

spider crab

ninja shark

These animals make light	These animals have a shell
angler fish	

14 Look at the picture and read the questions. Write the answers.

1 What animal is this?

This animal is a giant squid.

2 How many tentacles has it got?

....

3 Do you think it is dangerous? Why? / Why not?

....

....

15 With a friend, ask and answer questions about fish at the bottom of the oceans.

1 *Which fish do you find at the bottom of the oceans?*

There are angler fish and gulper eels at the bottom of the oceans.

2 What kind of water do these fish like?

3 How are these fish different from other fish?

16 Do the crossword.

			¹f	²o	o	d
		³l				
⁴h						

⁵s

Across

1 A ninja shark's skin changes when it is looking for . . .

4 A ninja shark's skin helps it to . . . from other fish.

5 A ninja . . . was first found in the Pacific Ocean.

Down

2 New animals are still found in the . . .

3 A ninja shark has dark skin that becomes a . . . in the dark ocean.

17 **Circle the correct words.**

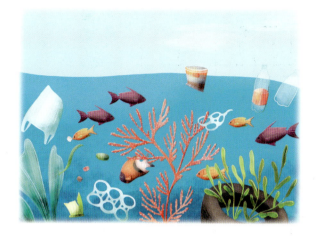

1 There are many problems for the animals and plants that live in the (oceans.) / oshans.

2 We must not **catch** / **cach** too many fish!

3 One of the biggest problems in the oceans is **garbage.** / **garbege.**

4 Garbage is the things **people** / **peeple** don't want.

5 Fish eat garbage in the oceans **becus** / **because** it looks good to eat.

18 **Read the answers. Write the questions.**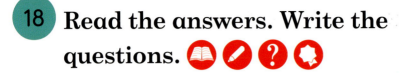

1 <u>Why shouldn't people catch as many fish as they like?</u>
Because there will be no more fish in the future.

2 ....

....?

No, but they should not eat a lot of them.

3 ....

....?

We have to clean them, or we may lose all the animals and plants that live in them.

19 Write *clean* or *cleaning*.

1 All of us can _____ clean _____ our beaches and the oceans.

2 We could make a _____ machine like this.

3 This machine could _____ the oceans. It can find garbage in the water.

4 If we don't start _____ our oceans, our world will have many problems.

Level 4

The Pied Piper of Hamelin

978–0–241–25378–6

The Wizard of Oz

978–0–241–25379–3

Sam and the Robots

978–0–241–25380–9

The Little Mermaid

978–0–241–29874–9

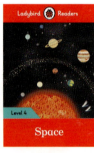

Space

978–0–241–25381–6

Pinocchio

978–0–241–28430–8

Alice in Wonderland

978–0–241–28431–5

Under the Oceans

978–0–241–29888–6

Knights and Castles

978–0–241–28432–2

Heidi

978–0–241–28433–9

Peter and the Wolf

978–0–241–28434–6

Dangerous Journeys

978–0–241–29891–6

A Fight with Underbite

978-0-241-29890-9

Sideswipe Loses his Head

978-0-241-29889-3